POMANDO

OTHER BOOKS BY M. JEAN CRAIG

Boxes
The Dragon in the Clock Box
New Boy on the Sidewalk
Not Very Much of a House
The Long and Dangerous Journey

POMANDO

by M. Jean Craig

Illustrated by Enrico Arno

W · W · Norton & Company · Inc ·
New York

POMANDO

I

ONCE, IN A LAND VERY FAR from here, and at a time much earlier than now, there was a kingdom called Yolalia. In this kingdom lived a poor, hungry young painter. His name was Pomando.

Pomando painted beautiful pictures of beautiful things. He painted pictures of all the beautiful things he imagined in his head and saw in his heart. He worked hard and he worked well, and it is perhaps difficult to believe that anyone who works hard and well should be poor, or have to go hungry, but Pomando was and Pomando did. He almost always went hungry at breakfast-time and he very often went hungry at lunch-time and he quite frequently went hungry at dinner-time. He went hungry so much of the time because he was so poor. And he was so poor because no one in Yolalia would buy his pictures.

In fact, no one in Yolalia even liked his pictures.

In fact, no one in Yolalia even wanted to look at his pictures.

"You paint things that aren't real, so I won't buy them," people said.

"You paint things that I've never seen, so I don't like them," people said.

"You paint things that make me somehow wanting-ish, and sad, so I won't even look at them," people said.

"Why don't you paint real things?" people asked. "Why don't you paint what is real?"

"I do paint real things," Pomando always answered. "I paint what is real to me. I paint what I see."

Then he would look into his heart and

into his head, and he would pick up his paintbrush and paint some more.

Now the truth is that the people who lived in Yolalia were perfectly right. None of the beautiful pictures that Pomando painted could possibly have seemed real to them. The truth is that . . .

> there was not a single thing in all of
> Yolalia that *was* beautiful, so
> not a single person in Yolalia had ever
> seen a beautiful thing *in* Yolalia, and
> not a single person in Yolalia had ever
> seen anything at all *not* in Yolalia, so
> *not a single person in Yolalia had ever*
> *seen a single beautiful thing.*

Perhaps that is difficult to believe, too, but it is really and truly true. To understand how it could be true, you would have to understand what Yolalia was like.

2

YOLALIA WAS, FIRST OF ALL, A very little kingdom. It was not quite as big as the smallest of the very littlest countries that exist in the world today. It was only big enough to cover a very small flat place on the very top of a very high (but very thin) mountain.

Next, Yolalia was a very old kingdom. It was so old that no one knew when it had been built. It was so old that some Yolalians believed it had never been built at all, but had always just been there. All the people who lived in Yolalia in Pomando's time had been born there, and so had their fathers and their mothers, and so had the mothers and the fathers of their fathers and their mothers, and so had *their* fathers and *their* mothers, and so had and so had and so had and so had, all the way back as far as time went.

Finally, Yolalia had a thick, high wall all around the whole edge of it, without one single gate or one door or even one little peephole of a window. Whoever had built Yolalia (if anyone ever had, if it had not always just been there) —whoever *might* have built Yolalia had taken all the stones left over from making the houses and the castle and the shops and the factories, and had used them to make the wall. Perhaps he had filled in the spaces for windows and doors and gates because he hadn't wanted to waste the last few extra stones. Or perhaps he hadn't liked to leave untidy heaps of loose stones lying around for someone to trip over. Whichever, the wall was absolutely smooth and solid, around and around and around.

And it was, all things considered, an excellent wall. Not a beautiful wall, of course, but an excellent wall. It was too strong to break down and it was too thick to see through and it was too high to climb over. (Most walls are like that. Walls are *supposed* to be like that, aren't they?)

With such an excellent wall, none of the people who lived in Yolalia ever left it, because they couldn't. With such an excellent wall, no people who lived anywhere else ever came to visit, because they couldn't. (That's what walls are for, isn't it?)

But no one in Yolalia minded that the wall kept them from going out or kept anyone else from coming in. No one in Yolalia had ever stopped to think that there might *be* anyone or anyplace else. To tell the whole truth, no one in Yolalia ever noticed that a wall was there at all.

"Wall? Out? In? Else? What are you talking about?" That is what anyone in Yolalia might have said if his attention had been called to the wall.

Inside the wall, at the time of this story, lived exactly seven hundred and forty-two Yolalians, including Pomando, the hungry young painter. In fact, at any time and at all times there were always exactly seven hundred and forty-two Yolalians living in Yolalia, never any more, never any less. Every time someone's baby was born, someone else's grandmother, or great-grandfather, or elderly-third-cousin-once-removed, would die. This worked out very neatly.

Furthermore, there were always just enough boys and girls born to each family —one of each to each family was the way it always was—for every young woman to find a husband and for every young man to find a wife, when the right time came. Considering the size of the country, and also the excellence of its wall, this worked out very neatly too.

Actually, everything in Yolalia worked out very neatly. There were just enough houses for seven hundred and forty-two Yolalians to live in. There were just enough factories to make their food and their clothing and all the other things they needed. There were just enough shops to sell what the factories made. There were just enough workmen to repair what the shops sold. And so on. All very neat, and quite comfortable, and just so, and nothing extra, and nothing not enough, and no loose ends.

And nothing—not one single solitary thing—in the whole kingdom that was beautiful.

Now a kingdom with such an excellent
wall all the way around it doesn't absolutely
have to be a kingdom where nothing at all
is beautiful, but there is no doubt that such
a wall helps. With such a wall, for instance,
one can never Look Out. Because of the
wall, no one in Yolalia had ever seen, for
example, the dark, tall pines that grew on
the sides of the mountains, or the wide
green fields at the bottom of the valleys, or
the flower-strewn meadows with small
brown streams curving through them. Naturally there were no trees or fields or meadows or small brown streams inside the wall
of Yolalia, because there wasn't room for
them. There was room only for seven hundred and forty-two Yolalians and their
houses and their factories and their shops
and their castle. There were no flowers in
Yolalia, either, nor even weeds, nor any
green thing growing. If something green
began to grow from a crack between the
cobblestones (from a seed blown from hea-
ven knew where), the first Yolalian who

saw it would pull it out quickly, because it didn't seem to belong there.

Even with such an excellent wall, it is usually possible, of course, to Look Up. When one Looks Up, there is the golden sun and there is the blue sky, both of which are quite beautiful. At night there is the silver-gold moon and there are the stars, and the moon and the stars are considered by some people to be very beautiful indeed.

But Yolalians couldn't even Look Up. Or, that is, they could look *up,* but not very far, and not as far as *Up.* The factories in Yolalia had to run all of the time to make all of the food and the clothing and the other things that the Yolalians needed, and thick gray smoke rose from their chimneys twenty-four hours a day. It blotted out the golden sun and the blue sky and the silver-gold moon and the stars. No one living in Yolalia had ever seen them, any of them. Yolalians had never Looked Up any more than they had Looked Out. Yolalians had never looked anywhere except at each other and at their houses and their shops and their castle and their factories.

Now the Yolalians were hard-working and honest and strong and kind and healthy, but they were not even a little bit beautiful—not any of them. When they looked at each other, there was nothing beautiful to see.

And their houses and their shops were well-built and serviceable, but not in the least beautiful. (It is hard, perhaps, for people who have never seen anything beautiful to make anything beautiful.)

The castle of Yolalia was not only not beautiful, it was really extremely ugly, of a muddy color and a clumsy shape. But no one knew this—except perhaps Pomando.

As for the factories of Yolalia—well, factories are hardly ever beautiful, even today, and this was a time *much* earlier than now.

That is what Yolalia was like, and that is why no Yolalian had ever seen anything that was beautiful. And that is why poor Pomando, who worked hard and well painting beautiful things, was scorned by the people of Yolalia and was almost always hungry.

3

THE KING OF YOLALIA, AT THE time of this story, was a contented sort of king, and he was almost altogether contented with his kingdom. There was just one thing he thought Yolalia lacked, and that was a Royal Artist.

"Any kingdom worth the name ought to have a Royal Artist," he would grumble mildly from time to time. "We have a Royal Builder and a Royal Tailor and a Royal Sweeper and a Royal Cook. It is not right that we have no Royal Artist."

Then one morning the King learned that there was, in fact, a painter living in Yolalia, something he somehow hadn't known before. He scolded all the people who hadn't told him, asked where Pomando could be found, and went immediately to visit him.

Pomando's tiny cottage was backed right up against the wall on the eastern edge of Yolalia. When the King arrived Pomando was standing on his doorstep, looking off at nothing. He had just finished making a painting and he was waiting for another painting to come into his head.

The King said hello and Pomando said hello. And then the King, who was not the kind of king who talked in circles when straight lines were handy, said, "I am here to ask you whether you would like to be the Royal Artist."

Pomando was not the kind of young man to think in circles, either, when straight lines were needed (although he very much enjoyed thinking in circles, and in spirals too, just for fun). Now straight lines were needed, so, straight as a string, his thoughts came: "Yes certainly I would like to be the

Royal Artist because Royal Artists get paid
and then I would not be so poor and I
could stop going hungry at breakfast-lunch-
and-dinner-time and I might even be able
to manage a few snacks."

(No one must blame Pomando for thinking more about his empty stomach at this
moment than about the tremendous honor
of being the Royal Artist. He was really very
hungry, from almost no food yesterday or
today and from knowing there would probably be no food at all tomorrow.)

Before he could answer the King, Pomando had to swallow the wetness that was
suddenly in his mouth from thinking about
snacks. But then he answered at once, "Yes,
thank you, I should like very much to be
the Royal Artist."

"Then the Matter is Settled," said the
King, who liked Matters to be Settled.
"Now let me see your paintings."

Pomando stepped down from his doorstep, bowed, politely waved the King

through the narrow doorway of the cottage, stepped up again, and followed him inside.

Aside from a bed and a table and a chair and a stove, a cold stove, there was nothing much inside the cottage. Except paintings, of course. There were quite a few paintings.

There were paintings on all four walls. They hung from ceiling to floor and covered every inch of wall space except for the two windows and the doors, and they were so close together that no one could possibly guess what the walls themselves were made of.

There were paintings on the floor, standing on edge and leaning against the walls all the way around the room.

There were paintings stacked up two feet high on the tabletop, and there were paintings piled up three feet high underneath the table.

There were paintings propped against the chair and the stove, and there were paintings spread all over the bed.

The King of Yolalia looked up and down and all around. He beamed. Here was a Royal Artist indeed!

Then the King of Yolalia began to look *at* the paintings themselves. His broad smile vanished.

"Oh, dear," said the King of Yolalia. "Oh, dear. Perhaps the Matter is *not* Settled."

Pomando didn't say anything, but he at once stopped thinking about snacks. Many people, after all, had looked at his paintings before.

Now the King of Yolalia was not a stupid man. He knew that there might well be more to a painting than can be found by just glancing at it for a second or two, or even three.

So he stared hard at one smallish painting on the wall for nearly a whole minute. Then he moved to the table and picked up another painting from the top of the stack and looked that one over carefully, for more than a whole minute. (It was a larger painting than the first one.) He ran a finger along its bottom edge. He tipped it flat and peered across its surface, first with his left eye and then with his right eye. He even brought it up to his nose and sniffed it, before he laid it down again.

He began to walk to the other side of the cottage to examine a third painting standing on the floor, but halfway across he stopped and shook his head.

"Oh, dear," said the King of Yolalia once more, and sighed, and turned to Pomando, who was still standing just inside the door-way.

The King of Yolalia was not a stupid man, and he was not an unkind one, either.

"It's not that you're a really *bad* painter, Pomando," he began, in a fatherly tone of voice. "Your paintings are very nice sizes, very nice indeed." The King cleared his throat. "And the canvas is well-covered with paint. I didn't see a single spot that you forgot to cover with paint." He cleared his throat again, and went on. "And I am glad —I might say I am extremely glad—that you know that paintings are supposed to be different colors. I notice that you use several different colors, and that's just fine. And even the edges of your pictures—they're just as straight and even as they can be. There's not a crooked edge in the lot, as far as I can judge without spending more time on them."

But then the King's voice grew stern. Even a kind man has to be honest. "The trouble is," the King continued, quite, quite sternly, "that paintings are supposed to be pictures of something real. What you paint is simply not real."

"I paint what is real to me," Pomando said, in a tired sort of way. "I paint what I see."

"Well, *I've* never seen such things," said the King indignantly, "and if they were real I would have." He pointed across the room. "That picture over there, for example, with all the odd green shapes at the bottom and the blue clearness at the top and the bits of thin white all wispy over the blue—now what, for example, would you call that?"

"That? Oh, well—that—that's a kind of— of distance," Pomando stammered. "That's a sort of—a sort of Looking Out. Yes," he went on more firmly, "that's a Looking Out. At Something Else."

"Distance? Out? Else? Meaningless—absolutely meaningless!" and the King's voice grew even sterner. "And so is this other nonsense—this bright yellowishness from the top coming down so that the little some-things below seem to—seem to glow or—I don't know what the little somethings seem to do, but they're not real in the least and what they seem to do is certainly not real in the least either!"

"They *are* real," said Pomando, hardly stammering at all. "And what they do is real too. It is a Reaching Up. For Other Some-things."

"Up? Up where? And for what other somethings? What other somethings are there?"

"The things I see. Beautiful things. Beau-tiful things the way I see them," answered Pomando, and his voice was strong now.

The King frowned, partly because he was very annoyed, but mostly because he was puzzled. "I don't know what you mean by—what was the word? beautiful?—but that hardly matters. What does matter,

Pomando, is that a painter must paint things that are real. That matters very much."

"But I do!" Pomando almost shouted. "I do paint real things, just the way I see them! The way I see them next to each other and far from each other and not with each other! I paint exactly what I see!"

"Well, then, *stop* painting what you see!"

"Oh, no!" said Pomando quickly. "I can't do that! I have to paint what I see. If I stopped, I'd stop being a painter at all!"

"Oh, no!" said the King, even more quickly. "You can't do that! You must not stop being a painter at all, or how can Yolalia have a Royal Artist?"

Then there was a silence.

The King thought hard, in a very straight line, about how Yolalia could have a Royal Artist *anyway*.

Pomando thought hard, in a very straight line, about how he could be the Royal Artist *anyway*. He also thought, in a little circle looping off to the side, about snacks.

At last the King's face brightened. "I know! If you have to paint what you see—and I do almost understand, I think, why that might perhaps be so—if you do have to paint what you see, then all you need to do is learn to see differently!

"Well—but——" Pomando began to stammer again, but the King was not listening. He was edging toward the doorway of the cottage, and talking very fast.

"No—no objections, Pomando, not a single word. I thought the Matter would be Settled at once, and, frankly, I am very disappointed. But you just learn to see differently as fast as you can, and as soon as you have . . ." and by then the King was gone.

Pomando finished his sentence for him. ". . . and as soon as I have, I can be the Royal Artist," he said softly, sadly, to the empty doorway.

And then he sighed, and pushed the paintings that were on the edge of the bed

into the middle of the bed, and sat down on the edge of the bed himself.

"All I need to do is learn how to see differently," he said to himself, "but how can anyone learn to see differently? That would be almost like Not-Seeing at all. That would be almost like Not-Knowing something you do know. Or Not-Loving something you do love. If you stay the same yourself, and if whatever you know or whatever you love stays the same itself, then you can't Not-

Know or Not-Love it, or do either one differently from the way you always have. And
I stay the same and the things I see, in my
head and in my heart, stay the same, so how
can I Not-See them or learn to see them differently?"

And Pomando sighed one more time, a
big long pulled-out sigh that came all the
way up from the soles of his feet.

Pomando spent the rest of the morning
sitting on the edge of his bed, Not-Finding
any answer to his question. At noontime
he went to his doorway and watched the
people hurrying by. Some were going here
and some were going there and some were
going home from work to have their lunch.

When he thought of lunch, Pomando
tried to pull his belt tighter, but there were
no more holes left to fasten it with. He decided to walk down the street to the cobbler's shop, and ask his good friend the cobbler to punch another hole in the belt for
him.

4

THE COBBLER OF YOLALIA didn't go home for lunch, but brought it with him every day to his shop and ate it there. When Pomando arrived, the cobbler was tilted back in his chair, just about to bite into a thick sandwich. He looked sharply at Pomando's face when Pomando laid his belt on the workbench.

"Yes, I'll be glad to do it for you, Pomando," the cobbler said, "if you'll do me a favor in return. My wife has given me three enormous sandwiches for my lunch again, and I am really having a great deal of trouble eating them all up. Perhaps you could eat this last one for me?"

"Why, yes," said Pomando. "I believe I could manage a sandwich right now." He picked up the sandwich, very slowly, and bit into it, very gently, and chewed the first mouthful, very carefully. And then, suddenly, onetwothree, the sandwich was gone. Pomando sat down and smiled at the cobbler and the cobbler smiled at Pomando and there was the kind of moment that comes sometimes between good friends.

The cobbler let his front chair legs thump down then, and reached for his eyeglasses and put them on his nose, and picked up the belt.

"If I put any more holes in it," he said. "I'm afraid we'll be all the way around to the buckle."

But Pomando wasn't listening. He was looking at the cobbler's eyeglasses. "Why do you put your glasses on when you start to work?" he asked abruptly.

"So I can see better, naturally," answered the cobbler, looking surprised.

"What do you mean, see better? See *differently*?"

"Why, I suppose you could say that. I'm getting older, and when I do close work everything gets a little blurry. The glasses make things clear again."

"Oh, let me try them! Do please let me try them!"

The cobbler laughed. "But, Pomando,

you're young, and your eyesight is perfect. Why do you want to wear glasses?"

Pomando told him the whole story, all in a rush. "So somehow, you see," he finished, "I must try to learn to see differently, so that when I paint what I see it will please the King, and then I will be the Royal Artist. And then"—he looked fondly at the cobbler—"and then perhaps you won't have to share your lunch with me so often."

The cobbler shook his head doubtfully, but handed his glasses to Pomando. Pomando put them on at once. He looked up at the ceiling. He looked down at the floor. He looked out through the small shop window into the street. He looked at his good friend the cobbler.

Then he slowly reached up and slid the glasses off and laid them down on the counter. "Everything looks blurry," he said. "But I can't really say I see differently. I just don't see well."

"Of course, those are *my* glasses, that

I chose myself for me," said the cobbler. "Maybe that is the trouble. People who wear glasses try on different pairs until they find a pair that suits them. There are many kinds of glasses in the eyeglass shop, and perhaps there is a pair there that will suit you."

Pomando was all out of breath when he reached the eyeglass shop, partly from running so fast and partly from excitement and hope and partly because he had left the cobbler's shop so quickly that he had forgotten to say either "Thank you" or "Good-by," and was embarrassed about this.

As soon as he got his breath back, he began to try on glasses. There were dozens of pairs of glasses in the eyeglass shop, on the counter and beneath the counter and in the cabinets that lined the walls.

First Pomando tried on glasses that had clear, round lenses.

Some made everything look blurry, the way the cobbler's glasses had.

Some made everything look sparkly and twinkly, which was rather nice for a minute or two but was very tiring after that.

Some of the glasses twisted everything into wrong shapes. "That's different," Pomando muttered, "but it isn't a good kind of different, or a real kind, and I can't paint it."

Some of the glasses made everything small and some made everything big, but not in the least different otherwise. "Small or big won't do any good," Pomando mumbled. "The King *liked* the sizes of my paintings. He said he did."

When Pomando had finished trying on all the eyeglasses with clear, round lenses, he began to work through the ones that had lenses of different colors. Some were yellow-brown, and some were a sort of gray, and a few were green. There were two pairs with blue lenses. The glasses with colored lenses made everything look yellow-brown, or a sort of gray, or green, or blue.

"That is quite interesting," Pomando

thought. "Everything I see is a different color, but otherwise I don't see differently. And besides," he remembered, "the King *liked* the colors of my paintings. He said he did. At least I think he said he did."

So he put the glasses with lenses of different colors aside and reached for a tray of glasses with lenses of different shapes. (They weren't really lenses though; they were only bits of window-glass. They were for people who didn't really need glasses but who just liked to wear them.) Some of these glasses had egg-shaped lenses and some had square lenses and some had lenses like tear-drops and one pair even had lenses in the shape of triangles. One after another, Pomando tried them all on. He certainly *looked* different when he was wearing them, but he didn't *see* differently. He didn't see differently at all.

At the end of the afternoon, Pomando walked slowly back to his cottage. He climbed into bed at just about the same time that everyone else in Yolalia was sitting down to eat dinner. And the next morning he went back to painting beautiful pictures of all the beautiful things that he saw in his head and in his heart and in his own way.

5

TWICE AGAIN IN THE NEXT TWO
weeks the King came to see Pomando. Each
time, he stepped inside the cottage and
looked quickly at whatever new paintings
were hung or leaning or stacked or piled
or spread around.

The first time the King came he shook
his head, said only, "Well, keep on trying,"
and left.

The second time the King came he just
shook his head and left.

Several more weeks passed before the
King came a third time, and this time he
did not come alone.

It should be mentioned here that the

Queen of Yolalia had died the year before.
It hardly ever happened in Yolalia that anyone died before growing quite old, but it did
happen now and then, by ill luck or by accident. It was certainly ill luck, or perhaps
accident, that this time it had happened to
the Queen.

Before she died, the Queen had had two
children, first a girl and then, a good many
years later, a boy.

It should also be mentioned here that the
King and Queen of Yolalia always had one
girl and one boy, just as everyone else did.
When a Princess grew up she would marry
an ordinary young man of her own age and
stop being a Princess. When a Prince grew
up he would marry an ordinary young
woman of his own age and go right on being
a Prince. When both the King and the
Queen died, the Prince and his wife would
become the new King and Queen. This was
the way it had always been, and it worked
out just as neatly as everything else in Yolalia.

You will not meet the Prince of Yolalia in this story, because he was very busy being taught by his nurse how to talk, and how to eat with a spoon, and how to drink from a cup, and he had no time to pay attention to what was going on outside of the nursery.

But the Princess of Yolalia, who had just recently become a young lady, often went here and there with her father because he liked to have her with him for company.

And that is why, the third time the King visited Pomando, his daughter went along too, for company.

The Princess of Yolalia was just about Pomando's age. She looked very much like any young woman who lived in Yolalia: pleasant and healthy and not one tiny bit beautiful. She was, perhaps, even rather plain.

While the King looked at the paintings hung on the wall and the Princess looked at the paintings stacked on the table, Pomando looked at the Princess.

While the King looked at the paintings leaning against the stove and the Princess looked at the paintings spread on the bed, Pomando looked at the Princess.

While the King and the Princess looked at the paintings standing on the floor, Pomando looked at the Princess.

When the King mumbled, "Not yet, the fellow hasn't learned yet," and walked out of the cottage, the Princess looked at Pomando.

"You have been upsetting my father for many weeks," said the Princess.

"I have not been trying to," said Pomando. "I have even been trying very hard not to. That is, for a while I was trying not to. But now I don't know how to try any more."

"He says that you don't paint things the way they really are."

"That *is* the way they are, when I see them."

"Are they really?" asked the Princess curiously.

She turned to the picture that Pomando had finished that very morning. It was still propped up against the easel, and the paint was still wet. Across the bottom there was some soft green, with little bright spots of different colors in the green and some ripply brown twisting through it. Farther up was more green, but darker, and only at the sides, and slanting out toward the side edges. In the middle and up to the top and

all across the top there was a changing, melt-
ing blue. Where the blue touched the green,
and in a streaky line across it, there were
seven different kinds of red and they all
had a sort of light shining through them.

The Princess stepped closer to the painting and looked at it with her eyes squinted
half-shut. Then she backed away from it
and looked at it with her eyes stretched wide
open. Pomando moved nearer to the Princess and looked at her every single way he
knew how.

"Are they really?" the Princess asked
again, with her eyes still on the painting.
"Is that really the way things are when you
see them?"

"That is the way *that* picture is when I
see it," Pomando answered. "When I see it
in my head. Or in my heart," he added, and
suddenly he put his hand on his heart, as
though to make sure it was still where it
had always been.

The Princess turned from the painting

then and lifted her eyes to Pomando's face. He was standing very close to her, looking down.

"I—I wish something were that way for me," she said. "I think it's—it's—I think it's——"

"Beautiful?" Pomando said the word so softly that it was only a breath.

"I am not sure what that word means, but it sounds as though it ought to mean what I mean. Yes—beautiful. I think it is beautiful. The green—and the shapes—and the way they are together and not together. It is like looking—well—Out. Or perhaps more like reaching—well—Up. I mean—I don't know quite what I mean, but I wish——" And the Princess stopped.

"What do you wish?" asked Pomando. "Dear Princess, what do you wish?"

"I wish you could be the Royal Artist," the Princess said quickly, and spun around quickly, and ran quickly out of the door of the cottage and down the street after her father.

6

POMANDO DIDN'T HAVE TO
wait for even a whole second after the Princess had left his cottage for another painting to come into his head. Before the sound of her footsteps had quite died away, his paintbrush was in his hand. He had never before painted a picture of a person. He had never before wanted to paint a picture of a person. But by early evening he had finished a portrait of the Princess. After the last careful brushstroke, he moved back a few steps to see, from a little distance, what he had done.

"Oh, beautiful!" he breathed. "She's so beautiful!"

Early the next morning there was a light tap on Pomando's door. It was the Princess, and her father was not with her. When Pomando opened the door, the Princess began to explain that her favorite handkerchief seemed to be missing, and had she perhaps left it on Pomando's table? But when she got to the word "handkerchief" she saw the portrait, and the sentence was never finished. (It is also probable that the handkerchief was never found. It was certainly not on Pomando's table.)

The Princess stared and stared and stared at the painting. Pomando said nothing. He just stared and stared and stared at the Princess. As he watched her, and as she looked at the painting, her eyes grew larger and larger, and their color, which was a sort of ordinary medium-dull average brown, changed and deepened and began to shimmer.

At last, "Oh, beautiful!" the Princess breathed. "She's so beautiful!"

"Yes," said Pomando.

"Did you see her in your heart?" asked the Princess.

"Yes, she is in my heart," said Pomando.

"Oh, if only she were real! No one in all of Yolalia looks like that!"

"The Princess of Yolalia looks like that," said Pomando to the Princess of Yolalia. "That is a picture of you."

But this was something that the Princess

knew was simply not true. In the castle, swinging on a stand in a corner of her bedroom, there was a long mirror. The Princess of Yolalia knew very well what the Princess of Yolalia looked like.

"You must not say things that are not so," she scolded. "I am not like that at all. Her eyes—the color of her eyes, and the light in them——"

"Your eyes are exactly that color now," said Pomando, "and they have exactly the same light."

"But the shape her lips make—and the way her hair springs up and then flows back and down—and how she holds her head! And see how she stands, ready to take a step, as though wherever she takes a step, that is where she wants to go. As though—as though if she walked, it would be happy walking. Oh, Pomando, that is not the way I am!"

"It is the way you are. It is the way you can be. They are the same thing."

"The same thing? I don't understand."

"Can be is the *same* as are. Don't you see that?"

"Do you see that, Pomando?" The Princess spoke much more slowly now. "Is that what you see? Is that what you see when you paint, that can be is the same as are?"

"Yes, that is what I see."

"When you look at me, is that what you see too?"

"When I look at you, dear Princess," answered Pomando, "all I see is how you are. All I see is you."

Pomando hoped the Princess would stay a little while for a visit, but she suddenly seemed to become rather absent-minded. She didn't even hear three separate remarks that Pomando made, and she left the cottage in a very short time.

Back home in the castle, the Princess went directly to her bedroom and closed the door and pulled a chair around to face the long mirror in the corner. She sat down in the chair and began to think.

She thought and she thought and she thought, and while she thought she watched herself in the glass. Several times she turned her head to one side, then to the other, and peeped at her reflection from the corners of her eyes. Several times, still thinking, she stood up, turned right around, and peered at the mirror over her shoulder. Two or three times she walked slowly back and forth, watching herself as she walked. Then she sat down and thought harder than ever.

"Whatever he says," was one of the things she thought first, "that is just not the way I am."

"But he said," she reminded herself a little later, "that it's the way I can be."

And right after that she remembered, "And can be is the same as are."

And then many times and over and over, she said out loud, "Can be is the same as are. There is no difference. They are the same. Can be is the same as are. Can be is the same as are. They are the same, the very same."

As the hours passed, some new thoughts began to come.

"If that's the way I can be, then I *can* be that way. There must be a way to try. Maybe I can find the way to try."

"The way to try is to practice," was the next new thought. "I could practice!"

"But practice what?" the Princess wondered. "Practice how? How can one practice being beautiful?"

Then the Princess thought harder than she ever had in her life. And finally, at the very end of the long, long day, she came to the very end of that day's thinking: "I will practice being beautiful by feeling what beautiful is. I will practice feeling beautiful every day, until I become beautiful, like the beautiful Princess in Pomando's painting. I will practice feeling beautiful until I am as beautiful as I *can* be, as I *am*, because they are the same, the very same."

And then the Princess, feeling tired and hungry and a little, tiny bit beautiful too, already, asked to have her dinner served to her in bed, and it was, and she ate it and went to sleep.

7

FOR MANY, MANY DAYS AFTER
that no one in Yolalia saw the Princess, because she stayed in her room with the door
locked. She asked for her meals to be left
outside, and only when the servant had
gone away would she take in the tray.

The servant became worried about her,
and several times, when she brought the
tray, she would ask through the door, "Are
you all right? Are you well?"

The Princess would answer, "I am very
well. I am just extremely busy."

Even the King, who was always extremely
busy himself with kingly affairs, and who
was not in any case an especially noticing

sort of man, at last realized that he had not seen the Princess for many, many days. He stopped at her door himself once to ask, "Are you all right? Are you well?"

"Yes, I am very well," the Princess answered. "I am working. I am extremely busy."

"Well, be sure to get plenty of exercise," the King called out through the keyhole. "Young people need plenty of exercise."

But the Princess was brushing her hair as hard as she could and didn't hear him.

At last there came a morning when the Princess stood for a long, long time before the mirror in the corner.

She saw the way her hair sprang up and then flowed back and down, and her eyes shone.

She saw the deep, shimmering brown of her eyes, and she smiled.

She saw the shapes her lips made when they moved, and the way she held her head, and how she stood.

She took a step toward the mirror, and she saw that she stepped as though wherever she went, that was where she wanted to go.

"Yes, I think so," the Princess whispered. "I *know* I feel, now, just the way Pomando's painting looks, and I *think* I look—I really do think that the picture in my mirror is like the painting too. I think so, but I am not quite sure."

The Princess suddenly could not wait a minute longer to be quite sure. She snatched her cloak from the wardrobe, unlocked her door, and for the first time in many, many days she left her room.

She hurried through the streets of Yolalia, running so quickly and so lightly that no one knew who was passing.

When Pomando opened the door of his cottage she hardly said good morning to him Her eyes flew to the portrait on the wall.

She might have been looking in her mirror.

"Oh, it is the same! The picture in my mirror is the same!" the Princess cried. She dropped her cloak to the floor and turned to Pomando. "Look, Pomando! Do look!"

"I am looking," said Pomando. "All I have had to look at these many, many days is your picture, and that has not been enough."

"But, see, Pomando, see how I have changed! I practiced and I practiced, and I look like the portrait now!"

"Dear Princess, you look exactly as you have always looked. You look the way you are."

Then, for the first time since she had entered the cottage, the eyes of the Princess met Pomando's eyes. What she saw in his eyes, shining there for her to see, made her blush, and what Pomando spoke of, then, made her blush again, and when, quite a bit later, she walked slowly back to the castle, she had a great many new things to think about.

8

ONLY SIXTY-THREE PEOPLE SAW the Princess as she walked slowly home from Pomando's cottage, but within a very short time all of Yolalia was buzzing.

"Have you seen the Princess?" people asked each other excitedly.

"You must see the Princess!" people told each other urgently.

"What has happened to the Princess?!?!" people marveled.

"Have you seen how she looks? Have you seen how she has changed?"

"Have you heard about the Princess? They say she is so—so——"

"What has happened?"

"What has happened?"

"The Princess has become so—so——"

"The Princess has become so—beautiful? Yes, the Princess has become beautiful!"

No one knows today who first used the word "beautiful," but everyone knew at once, on that day, that it was the right word. Before the day had come to an end everyone was saying, "The Princess is beautiful! The Princess is beautiful!"

In the days that followed, whenever the Princess appeared on the streets of Yolalia, all the people would come running from the houses and the shops and the factories to gather around her, and to smile, and to feel something moving in their hearts that they had never felt before.

Soon everyone in Yolalia had seen the Princess, and nearly everyone had felt the new feeling, and then they began to wonder. They began to ask themselves and each other why and what and how, which of course are wondering words. But they found no answers. Finally some of them asked the Princess herself.

"I practiced," the Princess told them happily. "I practiced, and I tried."

"Practiced? Tried?"

"Yes, to be like Pomando's painting. Pomando said that I could be, and that I *was*, and that they were the same. I wanted to be like the painting so much that I just had to try. I just had to!"

"Pomando? Could be? Was? The same? *What* was the same? Pomando? What painting? WHAT painting?"

It is easy to see that the only answers that the Princess could give to the people of Yolalia turned out to be simply new questions—and of course answers do behave that way sometimes. So one after another the people went to Pomando's cottage to learn, at least, WHAT painting.

Pomando had hung the portrait of the Princess right in the middle of the best wall of the cottage, partly covering some other pictures that seemed not very important to him now.

One by one, the people of Yolalia went to the cottage to look at the portrait of the Princess.

"Yes, it is true. The beautiful Princess is exactly like the painting," said one old man, and he went away to do some more wondering.

"Oh, yes, I see now! The beautiful painting is exactly like the Princess," said a young woman, and she went away to do some more wondering.

"Oh, yes, both beautiful and the same, just the same!" said all the people of Yolalia, one by one, the old women and the young men and the boys and the girls and even the littlest Yolalian children. "Beautiful, and just the same," they all said, and one by one they all went away to do some more wondering.

(Sometimes answers to why and what and how are not found just where you look for

them, or at once, but in another place and somewhat later.)

During the next days and while they were wondering, the people of Yolalia went back to Pomando's cottage again and again to look at the portrait of the Princess. And as long as they were there in the cottage anyway, they found themselves looking again and again at Pomando's other paintings too, including the ones that were partly covered by the portrait. One young factory worker even asked Pomando to tip the portrait up from the wall a little, so that he could see the left half of a painting that was partly covered.

Many of the people of Yolalia had seen Pomando's other paintings before, at one time or another, but now they looked *at* them, in a new way and much harder, and after they had looked *at* them they went away to wonder some more, in a new way too and even harder than before.

Some of the people of Yolalia, as they left the cottage, could be heard to say softly, "Real? Not real!" and some could be heard to whisper, "Not real? Real!" and some could be heard to say, quite loudly, just the word "Oh!" and some didn't say anything at all.

And then one day someone must have murmured, "If the Princess could change just by practicing. . . ."

And then someone must have added, ". . . if she could become beautiful just by trying. . . ."

And then someone else must have interrupted, ". . . beautiful like Pomando's picture because she wanted to be. . . ."

And then someone must have continued, ". . . and if could be really *is* the same as is, and can be really *is* the same as are. . . ."

And finally a whole lot of people were half-saying, all together:

". . . wonder whether other things. . . ."

". . . real things. . . ."

". . . in Yolalia. . . ."

". . . do you suppose that Yolalia could be. . . ."

". . . noticed Pomando's other paintings. . . ."

". . . if perhaps we changed this. . . ."

". . . the Princess changed, and now she's. . . ."

". . . maybe if we moved that. . . ."

". . . or fiddled a bit with these. . . ."

". . . shifted those a little. . . ."

". . . painted with colors. . . ."

". . . if this were red. . . ."

". . . or orange. . . ."

". . . or a different shape. . . ."

". . . or next to that. . . ."

". . . or. . . ."

". . . or. . . ."

". . . or. . . ."

The people of Yolalia never altogether finished saying any of these things, not any single one of them. This was partly because their own words and wonders kept interrupting them or because they kept interrupting each other, but it was mostly because they were suddenly too busy. They were busy changing some things and moving other things and shifting these that way and coloring those this way. They did this only a little at a time and slowly at first; but they did some every day and more every day, and then more and more quickly as each day passed and as it became easier and easier with practice and with trying.

One day, for example, a man took down his front door and made a new one with the

pieces of the door laid just so and fastened
together just so in a way that seemed good
to him. Then he painted the new door carefully, using two different colors, according
to the way the pieces of the door were put
together. When he had hung the door back
on the hinges, he stepped a little way into
the street to see how it was, and felt the new
feeling moving in his heart, and whispered,
"Beautiful. It's beautiful!"

Another day a Yolalian mother tied a red

ribbon bow in her daughter's dark hair, and saw how the little girl's green eyes sparkled and became greener, and hugged her and said, "You look just beautiful!" and the little girl's face sparkled then too and she laughed and ran outdoors to play. Everyone who passed turned to watch her playing, because no child in Yolalia had ever looked just beautiful before.

On still another day, in the afternoon, a Yolalian carpenter began to make a bench as he always had done, straight and strong and true and with no rough spots. But after it had been nailed together, he smoothed a curve with his tools across the front edge of the seat, and smaller curves down the legs, in a way he had never thought of doing before. When the bench was finished it was a bench such as no one in Yolalia had ever seen before. The carpenter ran out of his workshop into the street and shouted, "Come and see the beautiful bench I have made!" and the people did come, as fast as they could run. They crowded into the workshop, and their eyes moved along the curves of the seat and the legs, and their fingers reached out to pass along the curves, too, just as the carpenter's tools had done.

"What a beautiful bench!" all the people said. "The carpenter has made a beautiful bench!"

And one morning, as Pomando's good friend the cobbler worked at his table, he decided not to cut his shoe pattern as he always had. Instead he tried a new way, so that the seams of the shoes he was making would join together in a way that seemed better to him than the old way, more—well, more *beautifully* than the old way. When the cobbler had finished making the pair of shoes, tears sprang to his eyes.

"Who would have dreamed that a pair of shoes could be beautiful?" he exclaimed. "No one! . . . Except Pomando. I think Pomando might have dreamed it."

Just about everyone practiced. Just about everyone tried.

"Could be is the same as are," people told each other when they passed on the street, instead of saying only "Good morning."

"Can be is the same as is," people said, smiling, instead of only "Good evening."

And just about everyone went back, over and over again, to Pomando's cottage to look, again and again, at Pomando's paintings to be sure they were practicing and trying the right way.

Many people, as time went on, bought one or two of Pomando's paintings to take home with them, so they would not have to make the trip to the cottage so often. Because of this, Pomando didn't go hungry any more, not at breakfast-time, not at lunch-time, not at dinner-time. He was even able, now and then, to manage some snacks, and he threw away his old belt and bought a brand-new one from his good friend the cobbler.

Pomando, these days, was just as busy as everyone else. He was painting a good many new pictures, and he was spending many

hours every day with the Princess, talking with her about how things can be and
making all kinds of delicious plans. And
besides painting and planning, he was seeing and talking with many more *other* people than he had ever done before.

This was because almost everyone who
had just finished making something or
changing something or moving something
or fiddling with something or coloring something would say, "Run and fetch Pomando
quickly!" or "Do please go and ask the
Princess to come!" It hardly mattered which
one was sent for, because they nearly always came together anyway, walking hand
in hand.

"Yes," Pomando would say, or the Princess (because it hardly mattered which).
"Yes, it is beautiful. It's the way it can be,
and it's beautiful."

And then the person who had sent for
Pomando or the Princess would smile, and
Pomando and the Princess would smile, and

there would be the kind of moment that comes sometimes between good friends.

"Yolalia is becoming beautiful," the people said day after day, as they passed one another in the street.

"We are practicing. We are trying," all the people said. "And Yolalia is becoming as beautiful as Pomando's paintings!"

It was true. Yolalia was becoming beautiful. Green things were allowed to grow in Yolalia now, wherever seeds fell. At first this was because no one had time to pull them out. But then, as small shoots sprang up from the seeds and small leaves opened out from the stems and small blossoms unfolded between the leaves, everyone said, "Flowers are beautiful!" After that they planted seeds purposely, around their houses and in the square, and every evening, after their work was finished and before they went to bed, they spent a little time watching them growing.

Soon there came a time—it happened to

be on a Wednesday morning—when someone—it happened to be a street-sweeper—
looked up at the thick, dull, gray smoke that
was Yolalia's sky. "That is not beautiful,"
the street-sweeper decided, and he sat down
at once on the curbstone and figured out

a way to make the factories eat their own
smoke instead of spitting it out of the chimneys.

And so it came about that for the first
time in hundreds of years, perhaps for the
first time since the very beginning of time,

the people of Yolalia saw the day-blue of the sky and the changing white clouds and the round golden sun and the golden, golden sunshine.

"Are they real?" the Yolalians asked at first. "Can they be real?"

When it was night the people of Yolalia stayed outdoors and watched the glowing moon, and saw how its color changed (and its shape, too, when night followed night) as it moved majestically across the black-blue of the night sky.

And the people of Yolalia saw the stars.

"They are real! Yes, they must be real!" said the people. "They are real and oh! how beautiful they are!"

And then the people of Yolalia were quiet, and they found themselves looking out beyond the moon and between the stars. And inside themselves they felt a—well, one small Yolalian boy said, "It feels like a kind of Reaching. Like a kind of Reaching Up.

"Yes."

"Yes."

"Yes," said the people of Yolalia.

Now that the golden sun shone every day upon the pale, small flowers around the houses and in the square, they grew larger and brighter and sweeter. One day a yellow butterfly came, and then two more; another day there was a little green bird who sang.

And then, finally, only a few weeks later, a stonemason picked up his pick one day and suddenly swung it hard against the wall around Yolalia, the strong, thick, high, solid, excellent wall that had always, always been there. There was no special reason for him to do this except that it was a perfectly glorious day, with the great golden sun shining warmly in the sky and some small golden flowers shining warmly in the soft grass where he stood, and . . . well, perhaps it somehow seemed to him just the kind of day for a stonemason to swing his pick hard against something strong and thick and high and solid, even though he had never even noticed it before.

Crack! went the pick against the wall,

and a small piece of stone flew out.

Crack! went the pick again, and a much bigger piece of stone tumbled to the ground.

He was a very strong stonemason, the strongest in Yolalia, but all at once (perhaps because it was such a perfectly glorious day) he seemed to have a strength that even he had never had before.

Five more CRACKS!!!!! and the tip of the stonemason's pick went through the wall to —nothing. He jerked it out of the wall and dropped it to the ground. He put one eye against the small hole the pick had left in the wall and peered through. A moment later a loud shout rang out in Yolalia, the loudest shout ever heard in Yolalia, a shout loud enough to be heard by everyone in every house and in every shop and in every factory.

When everyone came running, the stone-mason was swinging his pick like a fury. Stones were flying right and left, and the hole in the wall was already big enough for a dozen people to see through at one time.

Down came the wall in chunks. No one who stood there made a sound. They just looked.

They saw mountains rising higher than mountains, with whiteness gleaming where they were highest.

They saw trees standing tall on the mountain slopes, trees of a hundred greens and a thousand shapes.

They saw deep valleys and broad meadows full of sun.

They saw harsh and wonderful stony cliffs and sandy, gentle shores.

They saw a wide blue winding river and small brown running streams, and they saw water falling, falling, into a handful of cloud.

There was up and there was down; there was out and there was away; there was else.

There was out and away; there was other.

There was Other and there was Else.

Pomando had somehow known all along, but now everyone in Yolalia could see that there was Other and there was Else.

And after the wall came down, Yolalia became even more beautiful, and more, and even more.

9

NOW THE TIME IT TOOK FOR Yolalia to become beautiful was really a rather short piece of time, as one measures the kind of time it *can* take for a kingdom to become beautiful. And during all of it the King of Yolalia had been extremely busy again with kingly affairs.

Also, it must be remembered that the King was not a particularly noticing sort of man. That is, he did usually notice how things *are*, especially if they were in a straight line, but he was not one to pay attention to the difference between how things are today and how they were yesterday, which is often a curving or even a circular kind of difference.

True, the King was aware of a certain new buzz and bustle in Yolalia, but then Yolalians had always worked hard and well.

True, he had remarked a sort of new glow in the air, but then Yolalia had never been really *dark*.

True, he *almost* noticed that there was no more wall around the Kingdom. At least, he noticed that *something* was not quite the same as it had always been, but he was too extremely busy to stop and think what. Being a king uses up a great deal of time and attention.

And as for the change in the Princess, it did occur to him that the Princess seemed to be looking uncommonly well lately. "Perhaps it is because she is taking so many long walks," the King told himself. "Exercise is so good for young people."

The King had not been able, though, to go to Pomando's cottage for a very long time, as one measures the kind of time it *can* take to find a Royal Artist. He had not forgotten that any kingdom worth its name needs a

Royal Artist; he had only put the Matter aside until other more important kingly affairs were Settled.

One morning, when that morning's kingly affairs were all Settled a whole hour before it was time for lunch, the King set off once more for Pomando's cottage. Through the sunny streets he walked, between the houses and the shops and the factories, and around the brightly colored flowerbeds in the middle of the square.

"How do you do," said the King to a housewife who was sweeping her front steps.

"Good day to you," the King said to some workmen who were hurrying about their jobs.

"Everyone looks uncommonly well these days," the King thought to himself. "They must all be getting enough exercise. And, of course, in every way Yolalia has always been a splendid place for people to live."

"Good morning," said the King to Pomando when he arrived at the cottage. Pomando had just finished a painting and was standing on his doorstep looking off at nothing, waiting for another picture to come into his head.

"Good morning," said Pomando to the King.

"I have come," said the King, "to find out whether you have learned yet to paint what is real."

Pomando smiled. "I do paint what is real, as I always have," he said. "I paint what is real to me. I paint what I see, exactly as I see it. As I always have."

"Yes, yes, I know, I know. We went over that the first time," said the King impatiently. "What I mean is, have you learned yet to see *differently?*"

"No, I have not," said Pomando. "I tried to, or at least I tried to try to. But I have not been able to."

The Kings's face grew very long. "But Yolalia must have a Royal Artist! I have never been more contented with Yolalia—

a fine kingdom, the very finest—except that we still have no Royal Artist!"

"I am sorry," said Pomando, and he was indeed very sorry to see the King so disappointed. "I am indeed very sorry, because I would still like to be the Royal Artist. Though of course I don't need to be the Royal Artist quite so much as I did the last time you were here." When Pomando said this he loosened his new belt just a little, from just a little too much breakfast. "But I have still not learned to see differently."

"Do you mean to say that after all this time you are still painting exactly as you did before?"

"Oh, no, I don't mean that," Pomando answered. "There is a kind of black-blue I didn't know about before, and I do now. There is a green I wasn't sure *was*, so I hardly ever used it, but now I know it *is* and I use it all the time. And before, I painted Looking Out—at distances, you know—but now I have found other distances beyond dis-

tances and between distances, and I am
beginning to paint them, too. And as for
Reaching Up—oh, there is simply no end to
Reaching Up, no end at all, so I can never
paint that exactly as I did before either. No,
I am not painting at all as I did before. But
painting differently isn't the same as seeing
differently, you understand. I still *see* exactly the same way, and I still paint exactly
what I see."

"No, I don't understand," said the King,
looking almost ready to cry. "I don't understand one bit. All I understand is that any
kingdom worth the name of kingdom must
have a Royal Artist!"

Pomando could not bear to see anyone so
unhappy, especially a King.

"Perhaps," he said hopefully, "as long as
you are here anyway. . . ." and he opened
the door of the cottage, not looking hopeful
at all.

"Well, perhaps," agreed the King hopefully, "as long as I am here anyway. . . ." and

he went into the cottage, not looking hopeful at all.

The walls of the cottage were covered
with paintings; the floor of the cottage was
covered with paintings; the table was stacked
with paintings; the bed was spread with
paintings; there were paintings standing on
edge and leaning against everything they
could lean against except the stove, which
was still too hot from breakfast. But apart
from that everything was the same as it had
been the other times the King had visited
Pomando.

"What a waste," sighed the King. "What
a great pity! So many paintings, and not a
single one. . . ."

Then the King began to look *at* the paintings. His face began to brighten. Slowly,
slowly, the King began to smile.

"Why, Pomando," said the King, "it
seems to me that you have been trying quite
hard. It seems to me that you must have been
practicing very hard indeed. It seems to me
that you have learned a great deal!"

"I——I——" began Pomando, but the King wasn't listening; he was looking.

"These paintings—they are real, quite real! Pomando, now you *are* painting what is real!"

"Yes, of course, but I always——" began Pomando, but the King went right on.

"Now just look at that!" the King exclaimed, waving toward a painting hung near the door. "Look at that picture of our valley, with the mountains slanting down on each side, and the trees growing on the mountainsides just the way trees do grow, and the sky so clear above, and the little white clouds blowing. Why, I saw little white clouds blowing like that—*just* like that, Pomando!—this very morning, from my own bedroom window."

"But—but that's the same painting—but you saw that old one——" Pomando began, but the King didn't hear a word.

"And this other one," the King went on in great excitement, picking up a small painting from the top of the stack on the table. "This picture of the sun shining down on the beautiful flowers in our square, and the flowers turning up to the sun—it's as real as it can be. Why, it is just as though I

were walking through the square again, as I did not half an hour ago. You *have* learned to see differently, Pomando. You have learned to see real things, as they really are!"

This time Pomando did not even try to speak.

The King looked up from the paintings on the table, and there before his eyes was the portrait of the Princess, hanging in the middle of the best wall of the cottage.

"Why, that is my daughter! You have even painted my daughter!" The King nearly burst with pleasure. "And you've done it beautifully, just beautifully! Why, I knew it was a picture of my daughter the minute I saw it! Why, that could be the Princess standing there herself! Why, it. . . ."

With a great effort, the King made himself calm down. It was time for Matters to be Settled.

"Pomando," said the King as calmly and as formally as he could, "it is clear that you have tried. It is clear that you have practiced. It is altogether clear that you have succeeded. You have learned to paint my beautiful kingdom exactly as it really is. You have even painted my beautiful daughter exactly as she really is. There is no reason why you should not be appointed the Royal Artist at once. Let us consider the Matter Settled."

"But ——" began Pomando.

"I paint what——" began Pomando, one last time, and then stopped. There was a very small but extremely busy silence.

Then, "Yes," said Pomando.

And, "Thank you," said Pomando.

"I should like very much to be the Royal Artist," said Pomando.

10

NOT VERY MANY MONTHS later, Pomando and the Princess were married, at which time, of course, the Princess immediately stopped being a Princess. She went to live with Pomando in his cottage, but it was a tiny cottage no longer. Pomando had built many new rooms with stones from the old wall, and now the cottage was a fine, large house. Every room had windows looking out across the valley to the distant mountains. From every window one could watch the golden sunrise in the morning and the silver-gold moonrise in the evening.

The King's ugly castle, of a muddy color and a clumsy shape, was torn down and a

new one was built in time for the wedding, a shining castle with smooth, cream-tinted walls and soaring spires and towers that gleamed like the tops of the mountains.

The portrait of the Wife of the Royal Artist was hung in the throne room, in the middle of the very best wall. And, although all of this happened a very long time ago, at a time much earlier than now, it is probably hanging there to this very day.